Binti

Also by Nnedi Okorafor

Who Fears Death
Kabu-Kabu
Lagoon
The Book of Phoenix

Younger readers
Zahrah the Windseeker (as Nnedi Okorafor-Mbachu)
The Shadow Speaker (as Nnedi Okorafor-Mbachu)
Akata Witch
The Girl with the Magic Hands
Long Juju Man

BINTI

Nnedi Okorafor

A TOM DOHERTY ASSOCIATES BOOK

NEW YORK

BINTI

Copyright © 2015 by Nnedi Okorafor

Cover art copyright © 2015 by Dave Palumbo

A Tor.com Book
Published by Tom Doherty Associates, LLC
175 Fifth Avenue
New York, NY 10010

www.tor.com

Tor* is a registered trademark of Tom Doherty Associates, LLC.

ISBN 978-0-7653-8446-1 (e-book)
ISBN 978-0-7653-8525-3 (trade paperback)

First Edition: September 2015

20 19 18 17

*Dedicated to the little blue jellyfish
I saw swimming the Khalid Lagoon that sunny day
in Sharjah, United Arab Emirates*

Binti

I powered up the transporter and said a silent prayer. I had no idea what I was going to do if it didn't work. My transporter was cheap, so even a droplet of moisture, or more likely, a grain of sand, would cause it to short. It was faulty and most of the time I had to restart it over and over before it worked. *Please not now, please not now*, I thought.

The transporter shivered in the sand and I held my breath. Tiny, flat, and black as a prayer stone, it buzzed softly and then slowly rose from the sand. Finally, it produced the baggage-lifting force. I grinned. Now I could make it to the shuttle. I swiped *otjize* from my forehead with my index finger and knelt down. Then I touched the finger to the sand, grounding the sweet smelling red clay into it. "Thank you," I whispered. It was a half-mile walk along the dark desert road. With the transporter working, I would make it there on time.

Straightening up, I paused and shut my eyes. Now the weight of my entire life was pressing on my shoulders. I was defying the most traditional part of myself for the first time in my entire life. I was leaving in the dead of night and they had no clue. My nine siblings, all older than me except for my younger sister and brother, would never see this coming. My parents would never imagine I'd do such a thing in a million years. By the time they all realized what I'd done and where I was going, I'd have left the planet. In my absence, my parents would growl to each other that I was to never set foot in their home again. My four aunties and two uncles who lived down the road would shout and gossip among themselves about how I'd scandalized our entire bloodline. I was going to be a pariah.

"Go," I softly whispered to the transporter, stamping my foot. The thin metal rings I wore around each ankle jingled noisily, but I stamped my foot again. Once on, the transporter worked best when I didn't touch it. "Go," I said again, sweat forming on my brow. When nothing moved, I chanced giving the two large suitcases sitting atop the force field a shove. They moved smoothly and I breathed another sigh of relief. At least some luck was on my side.

~

Fifteen minutes later I purchased a ticket and boarded the shuttle. The sun was barely beginning to peak over the horizon. As I moved past seated passengers far too aware of the bushy ends of my plaited hair softly slapping people in the face, I cast my eyes to the floor. Our hair is thick and mine has always been *very* thick. My old auntie liked to call it "ododo" because it grew wild and dense like ododo grass. Just before leaving, I'd rolled my plaited hair with fresh sweet-smelling *otjize* I'd made specifically for this trip. Who knew what I looked like to these people who didn't know my people so well.

A woman leaned away from me as I passed, her face pinched as if she smelled something foul. "Sorry," I whispered, watching my feet and trying to ignore the stares of almost everyone in the shuttle. Still, I couldn't help glancing around. Two girls who might have been a few years older than me, covered their mouths with hands so pale that they looked untouched by the sun. Everyone looked as if the sun was his or her enemy. I was the only Himba on the shuttle. I quickly found and moved to a seat.

The shuttle was one of the new sleek models that looked like the bullets my teachers used to calculate ballistic coefficients during my A-levels when I was growing up. These ones glided fast over land using a combination of air current, magnetic fields, and exponential energy—an easy craft to build if you had the equipment and the time. It was also a nice vehicle for hot desert terrain where the roads leading out of town were terribly maintained. My people didn't like to leave the homeland. I sat in the back so I could look out the large window.

I could see the lights from my father's astrolabe shop and the sand storm analyzer my brother had built at the top of the Root—that's what we called my parents' big, big house. Six generations of my family had lived there. It was the oldest house in my village, maybe the oldest in the city. It was made of stone and concrete, cool in the night, hot in the day. And it was patched with solar planes and covered with bioluminescent plants that liked to stop glowing just before sunrise. My bedroom was at the top of the house. The shuttle began to move and I stared until I couldn't see it anymore. "What am I do-ing?" I whispered.

An hour and a half later, the shuttle arrived at the launch port. I was the last off, which was good because the sight of the launch port overwhelmed me so much that all I could do for several moments was stand there. I was wearing a long red skirt, one that was silky like water, a light orange wind-top that was stiff and durable, thin leather sandals, and my anklets. No one around me wore such an outfit. All I saw were light flowing garments and veils; not one woman's ankles were exposed, let alone jin-gling with steel anklets. I breathed through my mouth and felt my face grow hot.

"Stupid stupid stupid," I whispered. We Himba don't

travel. We stay put. Our ancestral land is life; move away from it and you diminish. We even cover our bodies with it. *Otjize* is red land. Here in the launch port, most were Khoush and a few other non-Himba. Here, I was an outsider; I was outside. "What was I thinking?" I whispered.

I was sixteen years old and had never been beyond my city, let alone near a launch station. I was by myself and I had just left my family. My prospects of marriage had been 100 percent and now they would be zero. No man wanted a woman who'd run away. However, beyond my prospects of normal life being ruined, I had scored so high on the planetary exams in mathematics that the Oomza University had not only admitted me, but promised to pay for whatever I needed in order to attend. No matter what choice I made, I was never going to have a normal life, really.

I looked around and immediately knew what to do next. I walked to the help desk.

~

The travel security officer scanned my astrolabe, a full *deep* scan. Dizzy with shock, I shut my eyes and breathed through my mouth to steady myself. Just to leave the planet, I had to give them access to my *entire* life—me, my family, and all forecasts of my future. I stood there, frozen, hearing my mother's voice in my head. "There is a reason why our people do not go to that university. Oomza Uni wants you for its own gain, Binti. You go to that school and you become its slave." I couldn't help but contemplate the possible truth in her words. I hadn't even gotten there yet and already I'd given them my life. I wanted to ask the officer if he did this for everyone, but I was afraid now that he'd done it. They could do anything to me, at this point. Best not to make trouble.

When the officer handed me my astrolabe, I resisted the urge to snatch it back. He was an old Khoush man, so old that he was privileged to wear the blackest turban and face veil. His shaky hands were so gnarled and arthritic that he nearly dropped my astrolabe. He was bent like a dying palm tree and when he'd said, "You have never traveled; I must do a full scan. Remain where you are," his voice was drier than the red desert outside my city. But he read my astrolabe as fast as my father, which both impressed and scared me. He'd coaxed it open by whispering a few choice equations and his suddenly steady hands worked the dials as if they were his own.

When he finished, he looked up at me with his light green piercing eyes that seemed to see deeper into me than his scan of my astrolabe. There were people behind me and I was aware of their whispers, soft laughter and a young child murmuring. It was cool in the terminal, but I felt the heat of social pressure. My temples ached and my feet tingled.

"Congratulations," he said to me in his parched voice, holding out my astrolabe.

I frowned at him, confused. "What for?"

"You are the pride of your people, child," he said, looking me in the eye. Then he smiled broadly and patted my shoulder. He'd just seen my entire life. He knew of my admission into Oomza Uni.

"Oh." My eyes pricked with tears. "Thank you, sir," I said, hoarsely, as I took my astrolabe.

I quickly made my way through the many people in the terminal, too aware of their closeness. I considered finding a lavatory and applying more *otjize* to my skin and tying my hair back, but instead I kept moving. Most of the people in the busy terminal wore the black and white garments of the Khoush people—the women draped in white with multicolored belts and veils and the men draped in black like powerful spirits. I had seen plenty of them on television and here and there in my city, but never had I been in a sea of Khoush. This was the rest of the world and I was finally in it.

As I stood in line for boarding security, I felt a tug at my hair. I turned around and met the eyes of a group of Khoush women. They were all staring at me; *everyone* behind me was staring at me.

The woman who'd tugged my plait was looking at her fingers and rubbing them together, frowning. Her fingertips were orange red with my *otjize*. She sniffed them. "It smells like jasmine flowers," she said to the woman on her left, surprised.

"Not shit?" one woman said. "I hear it smells like shit because it *is* shit."

"No, definitely jasmine flowers. It is thick like shit, though."

"Is her hair even real?" another woman asked the woman rubbing her fingers.

"I don't know."

"These 'dirt bathers' are a filthy people," the first woman muttered.

I just turned back around, my shoulders hunched. My mother had counseled me to be quiet around Khoush. My father told me that when he was around Khoush merchants when they came to our city to buy astrolabes, he tried to make himself as small as possible. "It is either that or I will start a war with them that I will finish," he said. My father didn't believe in war. He said war was evil, but if it came he would revel in it like sand in a storm. Then he'd say a little prayer to the Seven to keep war away and then another prayer to seal his words.

I pulled my plaits to my front and touched the *edan* in my pocket. I let my mind focus on it, its strange language, its strange metal, its strange feel. I'd found the *edan* eight years ago while exploring the sands of the hinter deserts one late afternoon. "*Edan*" was a general name for a device too old for anyone to know it functions, so old that they were now just art.

My *edan* was more interesting than any book, than any new astrolabe design I made in my father's shop that these women would probably kill each other to buy. And it was mine, in my pocket, and these nosy women behind me could never know. Those women talked about me, the men probably did too. But none of them knew what I had, where I was going, who I was. Let them gossip and judge. Thankfully, they knew not to touch my hair again. I don't like war either.

The security guard scowled when I stepped forward. Behind him I could see three entrances, the one in the middle led into the ship called "Third Fish," the ship I was to take to Oomza Uni. Its open door was large and round leading into a long corridor illuminated by soft blue lights.

"Step forward," the guard said. He wore the uniform of all launch site lower-level personnel—a long white gown and gray gloves. I'd only seen this uniform in streaming stories and books and I wanted to giggle, despite myself. He looked ridiculous. I stepped forward and everything went red and warm.

When the body scan beeped its completion, the security guard reached right into my left pocket and brought out my *edan*. He held it to his face with a deep scowl.

I waited. What would he know?

He was inspecting its stellated cube shape, pressing its many points with his finger and eyeing the strange symbols on it that I had spent two years unsuccessfully trying to decode. He held it to his face to better see the intricate loops and swirls of blue and black and white, so much like the lace placed on the heads of young girls when they turn eleven and go through their eleventh-year rite.

"What is this made of?" the guard asked, holding it over a scanner. "It's not reading as any known metal."

I shrugged, too aware of the people behind me waiting in line and staring at me. To them, I was probably like one of the people who lived in caves deep in the hinter desert who were so blackened by the sun that they looked like walking shadows. I'm not proud to say that I have some Desert People blood in me from my father's side of the family, that's where my dark skin and extra-bushy hair come from.

"Your identity reads that you're a harmonizer, a masterful one who builds some of the finest astrolabes," he said. "But this object isn't an astrolabe. Did you build it? And how can you build something and not know what it's made of?"

"I didn't build it," I said.

"Who did?"

"It's . . . it's just an old, old thing," I said. "It has no math or current. It's just an inert computative apparatus that I carry for good luck." This was partially a lie. But even I didn't know exactly what it could and couldn't do.

The man looked as if he would ask more, but didn't. Inside, I smiled. Government security guards were only educated up to age ten, yet because of their jobs, they were used to ordering people around. And they especially looked down on people like me. Apparently, they were the same everywhere, no matter the tribe. He had no idea what a "computative apparatus" was, but he didn't want to show that I, a poor Himba girl, was more educated than he. Not in front of all these people. So he quickly moved me along and, finally, there I stood at my ship's entrance.

I couldn't see the end of the corridor, so I stared at the entrance. The ship was a magnificent piece of living technology. Third Fish was a Miri 12, a type of ship closely related to a shrimp. Miri 12s were stable calm creatures with natural exoskeletons that could withstand the harshness of space. They were genetically enhanced to grow three breathing chambers within their bodies.

Scientists planted rapidly growing plants within these

three enormous rooms that not only produced oxygen from the CO_2 directed in from other parts of the ship, but also absorbed benzene, formaldehyde, and trichloroethylene. This was some of the most amazing technology I'd ever read about. Once settled on the ship, I was determined to convince someone to let me see one of these amazing rooms. But at the moment, I wasn't thinking about the technology of the ship. I was on the threshold now, between home and my future.

I stepped into the blue corridor.

~

So that is how it all began. I found my room. I found my group—twelve other new students, all human, all Khoush, between the ages of fifteen and eighteen. An hour later, my group and I located a ship technician to show us one of the breathing chambers. I wasn't the only new Oomza Uni student who desperately wanted to see the technology at work. The air in there smelled like the jungles and forests I'd only read about. The plants had tough leaves and they grew everywhere, from ceiling to walls to floor. They were wild with flowers, and I could have stood there breathing that soft, fragrant air for days.

We met our group leader hours later. He was a stern old Khoush man who looked the twelve of us over and paused at me and asked, "Why are you covered in red greasy clay and weighed down by all those steel anklets?" When I told him that I was Himba, he coolly said, "I know, but that doesn't answer my question." I explained to him the tradition of my people's skin care and how we wore the steel rings on our ankles to protect us from snakebites. He looked at me for a long time, the others in my group staring at me like a rare bizarre butterfly.

"Wear your *otjize*," he said. "But not so much that you stain up this ship. And if those anklets are to protect you from snakebites, you no longer need them."

I took my anklets off, except for two on each ankle. Enough to jingle with each step.

I was the only Himba on the ship, out of nearly five hundred passengers. My tribe is obsessed with innovation and technology, but it is small, private, and, as I said, we don't like to leave Earth. We prefer to explore the universe by traveling inward, as opposed to outward. No Himba has ever gone to Oomza Uni. So me being the only one on the ship was not that surprising. However, just because something isn't surprising doesn't mean it's easy to deal with.

The ship was packed with outward-looking people who loved mathematics, experimenting, learning, reading, inventing, studying, obsessing, revealing. The people on the ship weren't Himba, but I soon understood that they were still my people. I stood out as a Himba, but the commonalities shined brighter. I made friends quickly. And by the second week in space, they were *good* friends.

Olo, Remi, Kwuga, Nur, Anajama, Rhoden. Only Olo and Remi were in my group. Everyone else I met in the dining area or the learning room where various lectures were held by professors onboard the ship. They were all girls who grew up in sprawling houses, who'd never walked through the desert, who'd never stepped on a snake in the dry grass. They were girls who could not stand the rays of Earth's sun unless it was shining through a tinted window.

Yet they were girls who knew what I meant when I spoke of "treeing." We sat in my room (because, having so few travel items, mine was the emptiest) and challenged each other to look out at the stars and imagine the most complex equation and then split it in half and then in half again and again. When you do math fractals long enough, you kick yourself into treeing just enough to get lost in the shallows of the mathematical sea. None of us would have made it into the university if we couldn't tree, but it's not easy. We were the best and we pushed each other to get closer to "God."

Then there was Heru. I had never spoken to him, but we smiled across the table at each other during mealtimes. He was from one of those cities so far from mine that they seemed like a figment of my imagination, where there was snow and where men rode those enormous gray birds and the women could speak with those birds without moving their mouths.

Once Heru was standing behind me in the dinner line with one of his friends. I felt someone pick up one of my plaits and I whirled around, ready to be angry. I met his eyes and he'd quickly let go of my hair, smiled, and raised his hands up defensively. "I couldn't help it," he said, his fingertips reddish with my *otjize*.

"You can't control yourself?" I snapped.

"You have exactly twenty-one," he said. "And they're braided in tessellating triangles. Is it some sort of code?"

I wanted to tell him that there *was* a code, that the pattern spoke my family's bloodline, culture, and history. That my father had designed the code and my mother and aunties had shown me how to braid it into my hair. However, looking at Heru made my heart beat too fast and my words escaped me, so I merely shrugged and turned back around to pick up a bowl of soup. Heru was tall and had the whitest teeth I'd ever seen. And he was very good in mathematics; few would have noticed the code in my hair.

But I never got the chance to tell him that my hair was braided into the history of my people. Because what happened, happened. It occured on the eighteenth day of the journey. The five days before we arrived on the planet Oomza Uni, the most powerful and innovative sprawling university in the Milky Way. I was the happiest I'd ever been in my life and I was farther from my beloved family than I'd ever been in my life.

I was at the table savoring a mouthful of a gelatinous milk-based dessert with slivers of coconut in it; I was gazing at Heru, who wasn't gazing at me. I'd put my fork down and had my *edan* in my hands. I fiddled with it as I watched Heru talk to the boy beside him. The delicious creamy dessert was melting coolly on my tongue. Beside me, Olo and Remi were singing a traditional song from their city because they missed home, a song that had to be sung with a wavery voice like a water spirit.

Then someone screamed and Heru's chest burst open, spattering me with his warm blood. There was a Meduse right behind him.

～

In my culture, it is blasphemy to pray to inanimate objects, but I did anyway. I prayed to a metal even my father had been unable to identify. I held it to my chest, shut my eyes, and I prayed to it, *I am in your protection. Please protect me. I am in your protection. Please protect me.*

My body was shuddering so hard that I could imagine

what it would be like to die from terror. I held my breath, the stench of *them* still in my nasal cavity and mouth. Heru's blood was on my face, wet and thick. I prayed to the mystery metal my *edan* was made of because that had to be the only thing keeping me alive at this moment.

Breathing hard from my mouth, I peeked from one eye. I shut it again. The Meduse were hovering less than a foot away. One had launched itself at me but then froze an inch from my flesh; it had reached a tentacle toward my *edan* and then suddenly collapsed, the tentacle turning ash gray as it quickly dried up like a dead leaf.

I could hear the others, their near substantial bodies softly rustling as their transparent domes filled with and released the gas they breathed back in. They were tall as grown men, their domes' flesh thin as fine silk, their long tentacles spilling down to the floor like a series of gigantic ghostly noodles. I grasped my *edan* closer to me. *I am in your protection. Please protect me.*

Everyone in the dining hall was dead. At least one hundred people. I had a feeling everyone on the ship was dead. The Meduse had burst into the hall and begun committing *moojh-ha ki-bira* before anyone knew what was happening. That's what the Khoush call it. We'd all been taught this Meduse form of killing in history class. The Khoush built the lessons into history, literature, and culture classes across several regions. Even my people were required to learn about it, despite the fact that it wasn't our fight. The Khoush expected everyone to remember their greatest enemy and injustice. They even worked Meduse anatomy and rudimentary technology into mathematics and science classes.

Moojh-ha ki-bira means the "great wave." The Meduse move like water when at war. There is no water on their planet, but they worship water as a god. Their ancestors came from water long ago. The Khoush were settled on the most water-soaked lands on Earth, a planet made mostly of water, and they saw the Meduse as inferior.

The trouble between the Meduse and the Khoush was an old fight and an older disagreement. Somehow, they had agreed to a treaty not to attack each other's ships. Yet here the Meduse were performing *moojh-ha ki-bira.*

I'd been talking to my friends.

My *friends*.

Olo, Remi, Kwuga, Nur, Anajama, Rhoden, and Dullaz. We had spent so many late nights laughing over our fears about how difficult and strange Oomza Uni would be. All of us had twisted ideas that were probably wrong . . . maybe partially right. We had so much in common. I wasn't thinking about home or how I'd *had* to leave it or the horrible messages my family had sent to my astrolabe hours after I'd left. I was looking ahead toward my future and I was laughing because it was so bright.

Then the Meduse came through the dining hall entrance. I was looking right at Heru when the red circle appeared in the upper left side of his shirt. The thing that tore through was like a sword, but thin as paper . . . and flexible and easily stained by blood. The tip wiggled and grasped like a finger. I saw it pinch and hook to the flesh near his collarbone.

Moojh-ha ki-bira.

I don't remember what I did or said. My eyes were open, taking it all in, but the rest of my brain was screaming. For no reason at all, I focused on the number five. Over and over, I thought, 5–5–5–5–5–5–5–5–5, as Heru's eyes went from shocked to blank. His open mouth let out a gagging sound, then a spurt of thick red blood, then blood frothed with saliva as he began to fall forward. His head hit the table with a flat thud. His neck was turned and I could see that his eyes were open. His left hand flexed spasmodically, until it stopped. But his eyes were still open. He wasn't blinking.

Heru was dead. Olo, Remi, Kwuga, Nur, Anajama, Rhoden, and Dullaz were dead. Everyone was dead.

The dinner hall stank of blood.

~

None of my family had wanted me to go to Oomza Uni. Even my best friend Dele hadn't wanted me to go. Still, not long after I received the news of my university acceptance and my whole family was saying no, Dele had joked that if I went, I at least wouldn't have to worry about the Meduse, because I would be the only Himba on the ship.

"So even if they kill everyone else, they won't even *see* you!" he'd said. Then he'd laughed and laughed, sure that I wasn't going anyway.

Now his words came back to me. Dele. I'd pushed thoughts of him deep into my mind and read none of his messages. Ignoring the people I loved was the only way I could keep going. When I'd received the scholarship to study at Oomza Uni, I'd gone into the desert and cried for hours. With joy.

I'd wanted this since I knew what a university was. Oomza Uni was the top of the top, its population was only 5 percent human. Imagine what it meant to go there as one of that 5 percent; to be with others obsessed with knowledge, creation, and discovery. Then I went home and told my family and wept with shock.

"You can't go," my oldest sister said. "You're a master harmonizer. Who else is good enough to take over father's shop?"

"Don't be selfish," my sister Suum spat. She was only a year older than me, but she still felt she could run my life.

"Stop chasing fame and be rational. You can't just leave and fly across the *galaxy*."

My brothers had all just laughed and dismissed the idea. My parents said nothing, not even congratulations. Their silence was answer enough. Even my best friend Dele. He congratulated and told me that I was smarter than everyone at Oomza Uni, but then he'd laughed, too. "You cannot go," he simply said. "We're Himba. God has already chosen our paths."

I was the first Himba in history to be bestowed with the honor of acceptance into Oomza Uni. The hate messages, threats to my life, laughter and ridicule that came from the Khoush in my city made me want to hide more. But deep down inside me, I wanted... I *needed* it. I couldn't help but act on it. The urge was so strong that it was mathematical. When I'd sit in the desert, alone, listening to the wind, I would see and feel the numbers the way I did when I was deep in my work in my father's shop. And those numbers added up to the sum of my destiny.

So in secret, I filled out and uploaded the acceptance forms. The desert was the perfect place for privacy when they contacted my astrolabe for university interviews. When everything was set, I packed my things and got on that shuttle. I come from a family of *Bitolus*; my father is a master harmonizer and I was to be his successor. We *Bito-*

lus know true deep mathematics and we can control their current, we know systems. We are few and we are happy and uninterested in weapons and war, but we can protect ourselves. And as my father says, "God favors us."

~

I clutched my *edan* to my chest now as I opened my eyes. The Meduse in front of me was blue and translucent, except for one of its tentacles, which was tinted pink like the waters of the salty lake beside my village and curled up like the branch of a confined tree. I held up my *edan* and the Meduse jerked back, pluming out its gas and loudly inhaling. *Fear*, I thought. *That was fear.*

I stood up, realizing that my time of death was not here yet. I took a quick look around the giant hall. I could smell dinner over the stink of blood and Meduse gases. Roasted and marinated meats, brown long-grained rice, spicy red stews, flat breads, and that rich gelatinous dessert I loved so much. They were all still laid out on the grand table, the hot foods cooling as the bodies cooled and the dessert melting as the dead Meduse melted.

"Back!" I hissed, thrusting the *edan* at the Meduse. My garments rustled and my anklets jingled as I got up. I pressed my backside against the table. The Meduse were behind me and on my sides, but I focused on the one before me. "This will kill you!" I said as forcibly as I could. I cleared my throat and raised my voice. "You saw what it did to your brother."

I motioned to the shriveled dead one two feet away; its mushy flesh had dried and begun to turn brown and opaque. It had tried to take me and then something made it die. Bits of it had crumbled to dust as I spoke, the mere vibration of my voice enough to destabilize the remains. I grabbed my satchel as I slid away from the table and moved toward the grand table of food. My mind was moving fast now. I was seeing numbers and then blurs. Good. I was my father's daughter. He'd taught me in the tradition of my ancestors and I was the best in the family.

"I am Binti Ekeopara Zuzu Dambu Kaipka of Namib," I whispered. This is what my father always reminded me when he saw my face go blank and I started to tree. He would then loudly speak his lessons to me about astrolabes, including how they worked, the art of them, the true negotiation of them, the lineage. While I was in this state, my father passed me three hundred years of oral knowledge about circuits, wire, metals, oils, heat, electricity, math current, sand bar.

And so I had become a master harmonizer by the age of twelve. I could communicate with spirit flow and convince them to become one current. I was born with my mother's gift of mathematical sight. My mother only used it to protect the family, and now I was going to grow that skill at the best university in the galaxy . . . if I survived. "Binti Ekeopara Zuzu Dambu Kaipka of Namib, that is my name," I said again.

My mind cleared as the equations flew through it, opening it wider, growing progressively more complex and satisfying. $V-E + F = 2$, $a^2 + b^2 = c^2$, I thought. I knew what to do now. I moved to the table of food and grabbed a tray. I heaped chicken wings, a turkey leg, and three steaks of beef onto it. Then several rolls; bread would stay fresh longer. I dumped three oranges on my tray, because they carried juice and vitamin C. I grabbed two whole bladders of water and shoved them into my satchel as well. Then I slid a slice of white milky dessert on my tray. I did not know its name, but it was easily the most wonderful thing I'd ever tasted. Each bite would fuel my mental well-being. And if I were going to survive, I'd need that, especially.

I moved quickly, holding up the *edan*, my back straining with the weight of my loaded satchel as I held the large food-heavy tray with my left hand. The Meduse followed me, their tentacles caressing the floor as they floated. They had no eyes, but from what I knew of the Meduse, they had scent receptors on the tips of their tentacles. They saw me through smell.

The hallway leading to the rooms was wide and all

the doors were plated with sheets of gold metal. My father would have spat at this wastefulness. Gold was an information conductor and its mathematical signals were stronger than anything. Yet here it was wasted on gaudy extravagance.

When I arrived at my room, the trance lifted from me without warning and I suddenly had no idea what to do next. I stopped treeing and the clarity of mind retreated like a loss of confidence. All I could think to do was let the door scan my eye. It opened, I slipped in and it shut behind me with a sucking sound, sealing the room, a mechanism probably triggered by the ship's emergency programming.

I managed to put the tray and satchel on my bed just before my legs gave. Then I sunk to the cool floor beside the black landing chair on the fair side of the room. My face was sweaty and I rested my cheek on the floor for a moment and sighed. Images of my friends Olo, Remi, Kwuga, Nur, Anajama, Rhoden crowded my mind. I thought I heard Heru's soft laughter above me . . . then the sound of his chest bursting open, then the heat of his blood on my face. I whimpered, biting my lip. "I'm here, I'm here, I'm here," I whispered. Because I was and there was no way out. I shut my eyes tightly as the tears came. I curled my body and stayed like that for several minutes.

~

I brought my astrolabe to my face. I'd made the casing with golden sand bar that I'd molded, sculpted, and polished myself. It was the size of a child's hand and far better than any astrolabe one could buy from the finest seller. I'd taken care to fashion its weight to suit my hands, the dials to respond to only my fingers, and its currents were so true that they'd probably outlast my own future children. I'd made this astrolabe two months ago specifically for my journey, replacing the one my father had made for me when I was three years old.

I started to speak my family name to my astrolabe, but then I whispered, "No," and rested it on my belly. My family was planets away by now; what more could they do than weep? I rubbed the on button and spoke, "Emergency." The astrolabe warmed in my hands and emitted the calming scent of roses as it vibrated. Then it went cool. "Emergency," I said again. This time it didn't even warm up.

"Map," I said. I held my breath, waiting. I glanced at the door. I'd read that Meduse could not move through walls, but even I knew that just because information was in a book didn't make it true. Especially when the information concerned the Meduse. My door was secure, but

I was Himba and I doubted the Khoush had given me one of the rooms with full security locks. The Meduse would come in when they wanted or when they were willing to risk death to do away with me. I may not have been Khoush . . . but I was a human on a Khoush ship.

My astrolabe suddenly warmed and vibrated. "Your location is 121 hours from your destination of Oomza Uni," it said in its whispery voice. So the Meduse felt it okay for me to know where the ship was. The virtual constellation lit up my room with white, light blue, red, yellow, and orange dots, slowly rotating globes from the size of a large fly to the size of my fist. Suns, planets, bloom territories all sectioned in the mathematical net that I'd always found easy to read. The ship had long since left my solar system. We'd slowed down right in the middle of what was known as "the Jungle." The pilots of the ship should have been more vigilant. "And maybe less arrogant," I said, feeling ill.

The ship was still heading for Oomza Uni, though, and that was mildly encouraging. I shut my eyes and prayed to the Seven. I wanted to ask, "Why did you let this happen?" but that was blasphemy. You never ask why. It was not a question for you to ask.

"I'm going to die here."

~

Seventy-two hours later, I was still alive. But I'd run out of food and had very little water left. Me and my thoughts in that small room, no escape outside. I had to stop crying; I couldn't afford to lose water. The toilet facilities were just outside my room so I'd been forced to use the case that carried my beaded jewelry collection. All I had was my jar of *otjize*, some of which I used to clean my body as much as possible. I paced, recited equations, and was sure that if I didn't die of thirst or starvation I'd die by fire from the currents I'd nervously created and discharged to keep myself busy.

I looked at the map yet again and saw what I knew I'd see; we were still heading to Oomza Uni. "But why?" I whispered. "Security will . . ."

I shut my eyes, trying to stop myself from completing the thought yet again. But I could never stop myself and this time was no different. In my mind's eye, I saw a bright yellow beam zip from Oomza Uni and the ship scattering in a radiating mass of silent light and flame. I got up and shuffled to the far side of my room and back as I talked. "But suicidal Meduse? It just doesn't make sense. Maybe they don't know how to . . ."

There was a slow knock at the door and I nearly

jumped to the ceiling. Then I froze, listening with every part of my body. Other than the sound of my voice, I hadn't heard a thing from them since that first twenty-four hours. The knock came again. The last knock was hard, more like a kick, but not near the bottom of the door.

"L . . . leave me alone!" I screamed, grabbing my *edan*. My words were met with a hard bang at the door and an angry, harsh hiss. I screeched and moved as far from the door as my room would permit, nearly falling over my largest suitcase. *Think think think.* No weapons, except the *edan* . . . and I didn't know what made it a weapon.

Everyone was dead. I was still about forty-eight hours from safety or being blown up. They say that when faced with a fight you cannot win, you can never predict what you will do next. But I'd always known I'd fight until I was killed. It was an abomination to commit suicide or to give up your life. I was sure that I was ready. The Meduse were very intelligent; they'd find a way to kill me, despite my *edan*.

Nevertheless, I didn't pick up the nearest weapon. I didn't prepare for my last violent rabid stand. Instead, I looked my death square in the face and then . . . then I *surrendered* to it. I sat on my bed and waited for my death. Already, my body felt as if it were no longer mine; I'd let it go. And in that moment, deep in my submission, I laid my eyes on my *edan* and stared at its branching splitting dividing blue fractals.

And I saw it.

I *really* saw it.

And all I could do was smile and think, *How did I not know?*

~

I sat in the landing chair beside my window, hand-rolling *otjize* into my plaits. I looked at my reddened hands, brought them to my nose and sniffed. Oily clay that sang of sweet flowers, desert wind, and soil. *Home*, I thought, tears stinging my eyes. I should not have left. I picked up the *edan*, looking for what I'd seen. I turned the *edan* over and over before my eyes. The blue object whose many points I'd rubbed, pressed, stared at, and pondered for so many years.

More thumping came from the door. "Leave me alone," I muttered weakly.

I smeared *otjize* onto the point of the *edan* with the spiral that always reminded me of a fingerprint. I rubbed it in a slow circular motion. My shoulders relaxed as I calmed. Then my starved and thirsty brain dropped into a mathematical trance like a stone dropped into deep water. And I felt the water envelop me as down down down

I went.

My clouded mind cleared and everything went silent and motionless, my finger still polishing the *edan*. I smelled home, heard the desert wind blowing grains of sand over each other. My stomach fluttered as I dropped deeper in and my entire body felt sweet and pure and empty and light. The *edan* was heavy in my hands; so heavy that it would fall right through my flesh.

"Oh," I breathed, realizing that there was now a tiny button in the center of the spiral. This was what I'd seen. It had always been there, but now it was as if it were in focus. I pushed it with my index finger. It depressed with a soft "click" and then the stone felt like warm wax and my world wavered. There was another loud knock at the door. Then through the clearest silence I'd ever experienced, so clear that the slightest sound would tear its fabric, I heard a solid oily low voice say, "Girl."

I was catapulted out of my trance, my eyes wide, my mouth yawning in a silent scream.

"Girl," I heard again. I hadn't heard a human voice since the final screams of those killed by the Meduse, over seventy-two hours ago.

I looked around my room. I was alone. Slowly, I turned and looked out the window beside me. There was nothing out there for me but the blackness of space.

"Girl. You will die," the voice said slowly. "Soon." I

heard more voices, but they were too low to understand. "Suffering is against the Way. Let us end you."

I jumped up and the rush of blood made me nearly collapse and crash to the floor. Instead I fell painfully to my knees, still clutching the *edan*. There was another knock at the door. "Open this door," the voice demanded.

My hands began to shake, but I didn't drop my *edan*. It was warm and a brilliant blue light was glowing from within it now. A current was running through it so steadily that it made the muscles of my hand constrict. I couldn't let go of it if I tried.

"I will not," I said, through clenched teeth. "Rather die in here, on *my* terms."

The knocking stopped. Then I heard several things at once. Scuffling at the door, not toward it, but *away*. Terrified moaning and wailing. More *voices*. Several of them.

"This is evil!"

"It carries shame," another voice said. This was the first voice I heard that sounded high-pitched, almost female. "The shame she carries allows her to mimic speech."

"No. It has to have sense for that," another voice said.

"Evil! Let me deactivate the door and kill it."

"Okwu, you will die if you . . ."

"I will kill it!" the one called Okwu growled. "Death

will be my honor! We're too close now, we can't have ..."

"Me!" I shouted suddenly. "O ... Okwu!" Calling its name, addressing it so directly sounded strange on my lips. I pushed on. "Okwu, why don't you talk to me?"

I looked at my cramped hands. From within it, from my *edan*, possibly the strongest current I'd ever produced streamed in jagged connected bright blue branches. It slowly etched and lurched through the closed door, a line of connected bright blue treelike branches that shifted in shape but never broke their connection. The current was touching the Meduse. Connecting them to me. And though I'd created it, I couldn't control it now. I wanted to scream, revolted. But I had to save my life first. "I am speaking to you!" I said. "Me!"

Silence.

I slowly stood up, my heart pounding. I stumbled to the shut door on aching trembling legs. The door's organic steel was so thin, but one of the strongest substances on my planet. Where the current touched it, tiny green leaves unfurled. I touched them, focusing on the leaves and not the fact that the door was covered with a sheet of gold, a super communication conducter. Nor the fact of the Meduse just beyond my door.

I heard a rustle and I used all my strength not to scuttle back. I flared my nostrils as I grasped the *edan*. The weight of my hair on my shoulders was assuring, my hair was heavy with *otjize*, and this was good luck and the strength of my people, even if my people were far far away.

The loud bang of something hard and powerful hitting the door made me yelp. I stayed where I was. "Evil thing," I heard the one called Okwu say. Of all the voices, that one I could recognize. It was the angriest and scariest. The voice sounded spoken, not transmitted in my mind. I could hear the vibration of the "v" in "evil" and the hard breathy "th" in "thing." Did they have mouths?

"I'm not evil," I said.

I heard whispering and rustling behind the door. Then the more female voice said, "Open this door."

"No!"

They muttered among themselves. Minutes passed. I sunk to the floor, leaning against the door. The blue current sunk with me, streaming through the door at my shoulder; more green leaves bloomed there, some fell down my shoulder onto my lap. I leaned my head against the door and stared down at them. Green tiny leaves of green tiny life when I was so close to death. I giggled and my empty belly rumbled and my sore abdominal muscles ached.

Then, quietly, calmly, "You are understanding us?" this was the growling voice that had been calling me evil. Okwu.

"Yes," I said.

"Humans only understand violence."

I closed my eyes and felt my weak body relax. I sighed and said, "The only thing I have killed are small animals for food, and only with swift grace and after prayer and thanking the beast for its sacrifice." I was exhausted.

"I do not believe you."

"Just as I do not believe you will not kill me if I open the door. All you do is kill." I opened my eyes. Energy that I didn't know I still had rippled through me and I was so angry that I couldn't catch my breath. "Like . . . like you . . . killed my friends!" I coughed and slumped down, weakly. "My friends," I whispered, tears welling in my eyes. "Oooh, my friends!"

"Humans must be killed before they kill us," the voice said.

"You're all stupid," I spat, wiping my tears as they kept coming. I sobbed hard and then took a deep breath, trying to pull it together. I exhaled loudly, snot flying from my nose. As I wiped my face with my arm, there were more whispers. Then the higher pitched voice spoke.

"What is this blue ghost you have sent to help us communicate?"

"I don't know," I said, sniffing. I got up and walked to my bed. Moving away from the door instantly made me feel better. The blue current extended with me.

"Why do we understand you?" Okwu asked. I could still hear its voice perfectly from where I was.

"I . . . I don't know," I said, sitting on my bed and then lying back.

"No Meduse has ever spoken to a human . . . except long ago."

"I don't care," I grunted.

"Open the door. We won't harm you."

"No."

There was a long pause. So long that I must have fallen asleep. I was awakened by a sucking sound. At first I paid no mind to it, taking the moment to wipe off the caked snot on my face with my arm. The ship made all sorts of sounds, even before the Meduse attacked. It was a living thing and like any beast, its bowels gurgled and quaked every so often. Then I sat up straight as the sucking sound grew louder. The door trembled. It buckled a bit and then completely crumpled, the gold plating on the outside now visible. The stale air of my room whooshed out into the hallway and suddenly the air cooled and smelled fresher.

There stood the Meduse. I could not tell how many of them, for they were transparent and when they stood together, all I could see were a tangle of translucent tentacles and undulating domes. I clutched the *edan* to my chest as I pressed myself on the other side of the room, against the window.

It happened fast like the desert wolves who attack travelers at night back home. One of the Meduse shot toward me. I watched it come. I saw my parents, sisters, brothers, aunts, and uncles, all gathered at a remembrance for me—full of pain and loss. I saw my spirit break from my body and return to my planet, to the desert, where I would tell stories to the sand people.

Time must have slowed down because the Meduse was motionless, yet suddenly it was hovering over me, its tentacles hanging an inch from my head. I gasped, bracing myself for pain and then death. Its pink withered tentacle brushed my arm firmly enough to rub off some of the *otjize* there. *Soft*, I thought. *Smooth*.

There it was. So close now. White like the ice I'd only seen in pictures and entertainment streams, its stinger was longer than my leg. I stared at it, jutting from its bundle of tentacles. It crackled and dried, wisps of white mist wafting from it. Inches from my chest. Now it went from white to a dull light-gray. I looked down at my cramped hands, the *edan* between them. The current flowing from it washed over the Meduse and extended beyond it. Then I looked up at the Meduse and grinned. "I hope it hurts," I whispered.

The Meduse's tentacles shuddered and it began to back away. I could see its pink deformed tentacle, part of it smeared red with my *otjize*.

"You are the foundation of evil," it said. It was the one called Okwu. I nearly laughed. Why did this one hate me so strongly?

"She still holds the shame," I heard one say from near the door.

Okwu began to recover as it moved away from me. Quickly, it left with the others.

~

Ten hours passed.

I had no food left. No water. I packed and repacked my things. Keeping busy staved off the dehydration and hunger a bit, though my constant need to urinate kept reminding me of my predicament. And movement was tricky because the *edan*'s current still wouldn't release my hands' muscles, but I managed. I tried not to indulge in my fear of the Meduse finding a way to get the ship to stop producing and circulating air and maintaining its internal pressure, or just coming back and killing me.

When I wasn't packing and repacking, I was staring at my *edan*, studying it; the patterns on it now glowed with the current. I needed to know how it was allowing me to communicate. I tried different soft equations on it and received no response. After a while, when not even hard equations affected it, I lay back on my bed and let myself tree. This was my state of mind when the Meduse came in.

"What is that?"

I screamed. I'd been gazing out the window, so I heard the Meduse before I saw it.

"What?" I shrieked, breathless. "I . . . what is what?"

Okwu, the one who'd tried to kill me. Contrary to how it had looked when it left, it was very much alive, though I could not see its stinger.

"What is the substance on your skin?" it asked firmly. "None of the other humans have it."

"Of course they don't," I snapped. "It is *otjize*, only my people wear it and I am the only one of my people on the ship. I'm not Khoush."

"What is it?" it asked, remaining in the doorway.

"Why?"

It moved into my room and I held up the *edan* and quickly said, "Mostly . . . mostly clay and oil from my homeland. Our land is desert, but we live in the region where there is sacred red clay."

"Why do you spread it on your skins?"

"Because my people are sons and daughters of the soil," I said. "And . . . and it's beautiful."

It paused for a long moment and I just stared at it. Really looking at the thing. It moved as if it had a front and a back. And though it seemed to be fully transparent, I could not see its solid white stinger within the drapes of hanging tentacles. Whether it was thinking about what I'd said or considering how best to kill me, I didn't know. But moments later, it turned and left. And it was only after several minutes, when my heart rate slowed, that I realized something odd. Its withered tentacle didn't look as withered. Where it had been curled up tightly into itself, now it was merely bent.

~

It came back fifteen minutes later. And immediately, I looked to make sure I'd seen what I knew I'd seen. And there it was, pink and not so curled up. That tentacle had been different when Okwu had accidently touched me and rubbed off my *otjize*.

"Give me some of it," it said, gliding into my room.

"I don't have any more!" I said, panicking. I only had one large jar of *otjize*, the most I'd ever made in one batch. It was enough to last me until I could find red clay on Oomza Uni and make more. And even then, I wasn't sure if I'd find the right kind of clay. It was another planet. Maybe it wouldn't have clay at all.

In all my preparation, the one thing I didn't take enough time to do was research the Oomza Uni planet itself, so focused I was on just *getting* there. All I knew was that though it was much smaller than earth, it had a similar atmosphere and I wouldn't have to wear a special suit or adaptive lungs or anything like that. But its surface could easily be made of something my skin couldn't tolerate. I couldn't give all my *otjize* to this Meduse; this was my *culture*.

"The chief knows of your people, you have much with you."

"If your chief knows my people, then he will have told you that taking it from me is like taking my soul," I said, my voice cracking. My jar was under my bed. I held up my *edan*.

But Okwu didn't leave or approach. Its curled pink tentacle twitched.

I decided to take a chance. "It helped you, didn't it? Your tentacle."

It blew out a great puff of its gas, sucked it in and left.

It returned five minutes later with five others.

"What is that object made of?" Okwu asked, the others standing silently behind it.

I was still on my bed and I pushed my legs under the covers. "I don't know. But a desert woman once said it was made from something called 'god stone.' My father said there is no such . . ."

"It is shame," it insisted.

None of them moved to enter my room. Three of them made loud puffing sounds as they let out the reeking gasses they inhaled in order to breathe.

"There is nothing shameful about an object that keeps me alive," I said.

"It poisons Meduse," one of the others said.

"Only if you get too close to me," I said, looking straight at it. "Only if you try and *kill* me."

Pause.

"How are you communicating with us?"

"I don't know, Okwu." I spoke its name as if I owned it.

"What are you called?"

I sat up straight, ignoring the fatigue trying to pull my bones to the bed. "I am Binti Ekeopara Zuzu Dambu Kaipka of Namib." I considered speaking its single name to reflect its cultural simplicity compared to mine, but my strength and bravado were already waning.

Okwu moved forward and I held up the *edan*. "Stay back! You know what it'll do!" I said. However, it did not try to attack me again, though it didn't start to shrivel up as it approached, either. It stopped feet away, beside the metal table jutting from the wall carrying my open suitcase and one of the containers of water.

"What do you need?" it flatly asked.

I stared, weighing my options. I didn't have any. "Water, food," I said.

Before I could say more, it left. I leaned against the window and tried not to look outside into the blackness. Feet away from me, the door was crushed to the side, the path of my fate was no longer mine. I lay back and fell into the deepest sleep I'd had since the ship left Earth.

~

The faint smell of smoke woke me up. There was a plate on my bed, right before my nose. On it was a small slab of smoked fish. Beside it was a bowl of water.

I sat up, still tightly grasping the *edan*. I leaned forward, and sucked up as much water from the bowl as I could. Then, still holding the *edan*, I pressed my forearms together and worked the food onto them. I brought the fish up, bent forward and took a bite of it. Smoky salty goodness burst across my taste buds. The chefs on the ship fed these fish well and allowed them to grow strong and mate copiously. Then they lulled the fish into a sleep that the fish never woke from and slow cooked their flesh long enough for flavor and short enough to maintain texture. I'd asked the chefs about their process as any good Himba would before eating it. The chefs were all Khoush, and Khoush did not normally perform what they called "superstitious ritual." But these chefs were Oomza Uni students and they said they did, even lulling the fish to sleep in a similar way. Again, I'd been assured that I was heading in the right direction.

The fish was delicious, but it was full of bones. And it was as I was using my tongue to work a long, flexible, but tough bone from my teeth that I looked up and noticed the Meduse hovering in the doorway. I didn't have to see the withered tentacle to know it was Okwu. Inhaling with surprise, I nearly choked on the bone. I dropped what was left, spat out the bone and opened my mouth to speak. Then I closed it.

I was still alive.

Okwu didn't move or speak, though the blue current still connected us. Moments passed, Okwu hovering and emitting the foul-smelling gasp as it breathed and me sucking bits of fish from my mouth wondering if this was my last meal. After a while, I grasped the remaining hunk of fish with my forearms and continued eating.

"You know," I finally said, to fill the silence. "There are a people in my village who have lived for generations at the edge of the lake." I looked at the Meduse. Nothing. "They know all the fish in it," I continued. "There is a fish that grows plenty in that lake and they catch and smoke them like this. The only difference is that my people can prepare it in such a way where there are no bones. They remove them all." I pulled a bone from between my teeth.

"They have studied this fish. They have worked it out mathematically. They know where every bone will be, no matter the age, size, sex of the fish. They go in and remove every bone without disturbing the body. It is delicious!" I put down the remaining bones. "This was delicious, too." I hesitated and then said, "Thank you."

Okwu didn't move, continuing to hover and puff out gas. I got up and walked to the counter where a tray had been set. I leaned down and sucked up the water from this bowl as well. Already, I felt much stronger and more alert. I jumped when it spoke.

"I wish I could just kill you."

I paused. "Like my mother always says, 'we all wish for many things,'" I said, touching a last bit of fish in my back tooth.

"You don't look like a human Oomza Uni student," it said. "Your color is darker and you . . ." It blasted out a large plume of gas and I fought not to wrinkle my nose. "You have *okuoko*."

I frowned at the unfamiliar word. "What is *okuoko*?"

And that's when it moved for the first time since I'd awakened. It's long tentacles jiggled playfully and a laugh escaped my mouth before I could stop it. It plumed out more gas in rapid succession and made a deep thrumming sound. This made me laugh even harder. "You mean my hair?" I asked, shaking my thick plaits.

"*Okuoko*, yes," it said.

"*Okuoko*," I said. I had to admit, I liked the sound of it. "How come the word is different?"

"I don't know," it said. "I hear you in my language as well. When you said *okuoko* it is *okuoko*." It paused. "The Khoush are the color of the flesh of the fish you ate and they have no *okuoko*. You are red brown like the fish's outer skin and you have *okuoko* like Meduse, though small."

"There are different kinds of humans," I said. "My people don't normally leave my planet." Several Meduse came to the door and crowded in. Okwu moved closer, pluming out more gas and inhaling it. This time I did cough at the stench of it.

"Why have you?" it asked. "You are probably the most evil of your people."

I frowned at it. Realizing something. It spoke like one of my brothers, Bena. I was born only three years after him yet we'd never been very close. He was angry and always speaking out about the way my people were maltreated by the Khoush majority despite the fact that they needed us and our astrolabes to survive. He was always calling them evil, though he'd never traveled to a Khoush country or known a Khoush. His anger was rightful, but all that he said was from what he didn't truly know.

Even I could tell that Okwu was not an elder among

these Meduse; it was too hotheaded and . . . there was something about it that reminded me of me. Maybe its curiosity; I think I'd have been one of the first to come see, if I were it, too. My father said that my curiosity was the last obstacle I had to overcome to be a true master harmonizer. If there was one thing my father and I disagreed on, it was that; I believed I could only be great if I were curious enough to seek greatness. Okwu was young, like me. And maybe that's why it was so eager to die and prove itself to the others and that's why the others were fine with it.

"You know nothing of me," I said. I felt myself grow hot. "This is not a military ship, this is a ship full of professors! Students! All dead! You killed everyone!"

It seemed to chuckle. "Not your pilot. We did not sting that one."

And just like that, I understood. They would get through the university's security if the security people thought the ship was still full of living breathing unmurdered professors and students. Then the Meduse would be able to invade Oomza Uni.

"We don't need *you*. But that one is useful."

"That's why we are still on course," I said.

"No. We can fly this creature ship," it said. "But your pilot can speak to the people on Oomza Uni in the way they expect." It paused, then moved closer. "See? We never *needed* you."

I felt the force of its threat physically. The sharp tingle came in white bursts in my toes and traveled up my body to the top of my head. I opened my mouth, suddenly short of breath. *This* was what fearing death truly felt like, not my initial submission to it. I leaned away, holding up my *edan*. I was sitting on my bed, its red covers making me think of blood. There was nowhere to go.

"That shame is the only reason you are alive," it said.

"Your *okuoko* is better," I whispered, pointing at the tentacle. "Won't you spare me for curing that?" I could barely breathe. When it didn't respond, I asked, "Why? Or maybe there is no reason."

"You think we are like you humans?" it asked, angrily. "We don't kill for sport or even for gain. Only for purpose."

I frowned. They sounded like the same thing to me, gain and purpose.

"In your university, in one of its museums, placed on display like a piece of rare meat is the stinger of our chief," it said. I wrinkled my face, but said nothing. "Our chief is . . ." It paused. "We know of the attack and mutilation of our chief, but we do not know how it got there. We do not care. We will land on Oomza Uni and take it back. So you see? We have purpose."

It billowed out gas and left the room. I lay back in my

bed, exhausted.

~

But they brought me more food and water. Okwu brought it. And it sat with me while I ate and drank. More fish and some dried-up dates and a flask of water. This time, I barely tasted it as I ate.

"It's suicide," I said.

"What is . . . suicide," it asked.

"What you are doing!" I said. "On Oomza Uni, there's a city where all the students and professors do is study, test, create *weapons*. Weapons for taking every form of life. Your own weapons were probably made there!"

"Our weapons are made within our bodies," it said.

"What of the current-killer you used against the Khoush in the Meduse-Khoush War?" I asked.

It said nothing.

"Suicide is death on purpose!"

"Meduse aren't afraid of death," it said. "And this would be honorable. We will show them never to dishonor Meduse again. Our people will remember our sacrifice and celebrate . . ."

"I . . . I have an idea!" I shouted. My voice cracked. I pushed forward. "Let me talk to your chief!" I shrieked. I don't know if it was the delicious fish I'd eaten, shock, hopelessness, or exhaustion. I stood up and stepped to it, my legs shaky and my eyes wild. "Let me . . . I'm a master harmonizer. That's why I'm going to Oomza Uni. I am the best of the best, Okwu. I can create harmony *any-where*." I was so out of breath that I was wheezing. I inhaled deeply, seeing stars explode before my eyes. "Let me be . . . let me speak for the Meduse. The people in Oomza Uni are academics, so they'll understand honor and history and symbolism and matters of the body." I didn't know any of this for sure. These were only my dreams . . . and my experience of those on the ship.

"Now you speak of 'suicide' for the both of us," it said.

"Please," I said. "I can make your chief listen."

"Our chief hates humans," Okwu said. "Humans took his stinger. Do you know what . . ."

"I'll give you my jar of *otjize*," I blurted. "You can put it all over your . . . on every *okuoko*, your dome, who knows, it might make you glow like a star or give you super-powers or sting harder and faster or . . ."

"We don't like stinging."

"Please," I begged. "Imagine what you will be. Imagine if my plan works. You'll get the stinger back and none of you will have died. You'll be a hero." *And I get to live*, I thought.

"We don't care about being heroes." But its pink tentacle twitched when it said this.

~

The Meduse ship was docked beside the Third Fish. I'd walked across the large chitinous corridor linking them, ignoring the fact that the chances of my returning were very low.

Their ship stank. I was sure of it, even if I couldn't smell it through my breather. Everything about the Meduse stank. I could barely concentrate on the spongy blue surface beneath my bare feet. Or the cool gasses Okwu promised would not harm my flesh even though I could not breathe it. Or the Meduse, some green, some blue, some pink, moving on every surface, floor, high ceiling, wall, or stopping and probably staring at me with whatever they stared with. Or the current-connected *edan* I still grasped in my hands. I was doing equations in my head. I needed everything I had to do what I was about to do.

The room was so enormous that it almost felt as if we were outside. Almost. I'm a child of the desert; nothing indoors can feel like the outdoors to me. But this room was huge. The chief was no bigger than the others, no more colorful. It had no more tentacles than the others. It was surrounded by other Meduse. It looked so much like those around it that Okwu had to stand beside it to let me know who it was.

The current from the *edan* was going crazy—branching out in every direction bringing me their words. I should have been terrified. Okwu had told me that requesting a meeting like this with the chief was risking not only my life, but Okwu's life as well. For the chief hated human beings and Okwu had just begged to bring one into their "great ship."

Spongy. As if it were full of the firm jelly beads in the milky pudding my mother liked to make. I could sense current all around me. These people had deep active technology built into the walls and many of them had it running within their very bodies. Some of them were walking astrolabes, it was part of their biology.

I adjusted my facemask. The air that it pumped in smelled like desert flowers. The makers of the mask had to have been Khoush women. They liked everything to smell like flowers, even their privates. But at the moment, I could have kissed those women, for as I gazed at the chief, the smell of flowers burst into my nose and mouth and suddenly I was imagining the chief hovering in the desert surrounded by the dry sweet-smelling flowers that only bloomed at night. I felt calm. I didn't feel at home, because in the part of the desert that I knew, only tiny scentless flowers grew. But I sensed Earth.

I slowly stopped treeing, my mind clean and clear,

but much stupider. I needed to speak, not act. So I had no choice. I held my chin up and then did as Okwu instructed me. I sunk to the spongy floor. Then right there, within the ship that brought the death of my friends, the boy I was coming to love, my fellow Oomza Uni human citizens from Earth, before the one who had instructed its people to perform *moojh-ha ki-bira*, also called the "great wave" of death, on my people—still grasping the *edan*, I prostrated. I pressed my face to the floor. Then I waited.

"This is Binti Ekeopara Zuzu Dambu Kaipka of Namib, the one . . . the one who survives," Okwu said.

"You may just call me Binti," I whispered, keeping my head down. My first name was singular and two syllabled like Okwu's name and I thought maybe it would please the chief.

"Tell the girl to sit up," the chief said. "If there is the slightest damage to the ship's flesh because of this one, I will have you executed first, Okwu. Then this creature."

"Binti," Okwu said, his voice was hard, flat. "Get up."

I shut my eyes. I could feel the *edan*'s current working through me, touching everything. Including the floor beneath me. And I could *hear* it. The floor. It was singing. But not words. Just humming. Happy and aloof. It wasn't paying attention. I pushed myself up, and leaned back on my knees. Then I looked at where my chest had been.

Still a deep blue. I looked up at the chief.

"My people are the creators and builders of astrolabes," I said. "We use math to create the currents within them. The best of us have the gift to bring harmony so delicious that we can make atoms caress each other like lovers. That's what my sister said." I blinked as it came to me. "I think that's why this *edan* works for me! I found it. In the desert. A wild woman there once told me that it is a piece of old old technology; she called it a 'god stone.' I didn't believe her then, but I do now. I've had it for five years, but it only worked for *me* now." I pounded my chest. "For *me*! On that ship full of you after you'd all done . . . done that. Let me speak for you, let me speak to them. So no more have to die."

I lowered my head, pressing my *edan* to my belly. Just as Okwu told me. I could hear others behind me. They could have stung me a thousand times.

"You know what they have taken from me," the chief asked.

"Yes," I said, keeping my head down.

"My stinger is my people's power," it said. "They took it from us. That's an act of war."

"My way will get your stinger back," I quickly said. Then I braced myself for the rough stab in the back. I felt the sharpness press against the nape of my neck. I bit my lower lip to keep from screaming.

"Tell your plan," Okwu said.

I spoke fast. "The pilot gets us cleared to land, then I leave the ship with one of you to negotiate with Oomza Uni to get the stinger back . . . peacefully."

"That will take our element of surprise," the chief said. "You know nothing about strategy."

"If you attack, you will kill many, but then they will kill you. All of you," I said. "Ahh," I hissed as the stinger pointed at my neck was pressed harder against my flesh. "Please, I'm just . . ."

"Chief, Binti doesn't know how to speak," Okwu said. "Binti is uncivilized. Forgive it. It is young, a girl."

"How can we trust it?" the Meduse beside the chief asked Okwu.

"What would I do?" I asked, my face squeezed with pain. "Run?" I wiped tears from my face. I wiped and wiped, but they kept coming. The nightmare kept happening.

"You people are good at hiding," another Meduse sneered. "especially the females like you." Several of the Meduse, including the chief, shook their tentacles and vibrated their domes in a clear display of laughter.

"Let Binti put down the *edan*," Okwu said.

I stared at Okwu, astonished. "What?"

"Put it *down*," it said. "You will be completely vulnerable. How can you be our ambassador, if you need that to stay safe from us."

"It's what allows me to hear you!" I shrieked. And it was all I had.

The chief whipped up one of its tentacles and every single Meduse in that enormous room stopped moving. They stopped as if the very currents of time stopped. Everything stopped as it does when things get so cold that they become ice. I looked around and when none of them moved, slowly, carefully I dragged myself inches forward and turned to see the Meduse behind me. Its stinger was up, at the height of where my neck had been. I looked at Okwu, who said nothing. Then at the chief. I lowered my eyes. Then I ventured another look, keeping my head low.

"Choose," the chief said.

My shield. My translator. I tried to flex the muscles in my hands. I was greeted with sharp intense pain. It had been over three days. We were five hours from Oomza Uni. I tried again. I screamed. The *edan* pulsed a bright blue deep within its black and gray crevices, lighting up its loops and swirls. Like one of the bioluminescent snails that invaded the edges of my home's lake.

When my left index finger pulled away from the *edan*, I couldn't hold the tears back. The *edan*'s blue-white glow blurred before my eyes. My joints popped and the muscles spasmed. Then my middle finger and pinky pulled away. I bit my lip so hard that I tasted blood. I took several quick breaths and then flexed every single one of my fingers at the same time. All of my joints went *CRACK*! I heard a thousand wasps in my head. My body went numb. The *edan* fell from my hands. Right before my eyes, I saw it and I wanted to laugh. The blue current I'd conjured danced before me, the definition of harmony made from chaos.

There was a soft *pap* as the *edan* hit the floor, rolled twice, then stopped. I had just killed myself. My head grew heavy . . . and all went black.

~

The Meduse were right. I could not have represented them if I was holding the *edan*. This was Oomza Uni. Someone there would know everything there was to know about the *edan* and thus its toxicity to the Meduse. No one at Oomza Uni would have really believed I was their ambassador unless I let go.

Death. When I left my home, I died. I had not prayed to the Seven before I left. I didn't think it was time. I had not gone on my pilgrimage like a proper woman. I was sure I'd return to my village as a full woman to do that. I had left my family. I thought I could return to them when I'd done what I needed to do.

Now I could never go back. The Meduse. The Meduse are not what we humans think. They are truth. They are clarity. They are decisive. There are sharp lines and edges. They understand honor and dishonor. I had to earn their honor and the only way to do that was by dying a second time.

I felt the stinger plunge into my spine just before I blacked out and just after I'd conjured up the wild line of current that I guided to the *edan*. It was a terrible pain. Then I left. I left them, I left that ship. I could hear the ship singing its half-word song and I knew it was singing to me. My last thought was to my family, and I hoped it reached them.

~

Home. I smelled the earth at the border of the desert just before it rained, during Fertile Season. The place right behind the Root, where I dug up the clay I used for my *otjize* and chased the geckos who were too fragile to survive a mile away in the desert. I opened my eyes; I was on my bed in my room, naked except for my wrapped skirt. The rest of my body was smooth with a thick layer of *otjize*. I flared my nostrils and inhaled the smell of me. Home . . .

I sat up and something rolled off my chest. It landed

in my crotch and I grabbed it. The *edan*. It was cool in my hand and all dull blue as it had been for years before. I reached behind and felt my back. The spot where the stinger had stabbed me was sore and I could feel something rough and scabby there. It too was covered with *otjize*. My astrolabe sat on the curve of the window and I checked my map and stared outside for a very long time. I grunted, slowly standing up. My foot hit something on the floor. My jar. I put the *edan* down and picked it up, grasping it with both hands. The jar was more than half-empty. I laughed, dressed and stared out the window again. We were landing on Oomza Uni in an hour and the view was spectacular.

~

They did not come. Not to tell me what to do or when to do it. So I strapped myself in the black landing chair beside the window and stared at the incredible sight expanding before my eyes. There were two suns, one that was very small and one that was large but comfortably far away. Hours of sunshine on all parts of the planet were far more than hours of dark, but there were few deserts on Oomza Uni.

I used my astrolabe in binocular vision to see things up close. Oomza Uni, such a small planet compared to

Earth. Only one-third water, its lands were every shade of the rainbow—some parts blue, green, white, purple, red, white, black, orange. And some areas were smooth, others jagged with peaks that touched the clouds. And the area we were hurtling toward was orange, but interrupted by patches of the dense green of large forests of trees, small lakes, and the hard gray-blue forests of tall skyscrapers.

My ears popped as we entered the atmosphere. The sky started to turn a light pinkish color, then red orange. I was looking out from within a fireball. We were inside the air that was being ripped apart as we entered the atmosphere. There wasn't much shaking or vibrating, but I could see the heat generated by the ship. The ship would shed its skin the day after we arrived as it readjusted to gravity.

We descended from the sky and zoomed between monstrously beautiful structures that made the skyscrapers of Earth look miniscule. I laughed wildly as we descended lower and lower. Down, down we fell. No military ships came to shoot us out of the sky. We landed and, moments after smiling with excitement, I wondered if they would kill the pilot now that he was useless? I had not negotiated that with the Meduse. I ripped off my safety belt and jumped up and then fell to the floor. My legs felt like weights.

"What is . . ."

I heard a horrible noise, a low rumble that boiled to an angry-sounding growl. I looked around, sure there was a monster about to enter my room. But then I realized two things. Okwu was standing in my doorway and I understood what it was saying.

I did as it said and pushed myself into a sitting position, bringing my legs to my chest. I grasped the side of my bed and dragged myself up to sit on it.

"Take your time," Okwu said. "Your kind do not adjust quickly to *jadevia*."

"You mean gravity?" I asked.

"Yes."

I slowly stood up. I took a step and looked at Okwu, then past it at the empty doorway. "Where are the others?"

"Waiting in the dining room."

"The pilot?" I asked

"In the dining room as well."

"Alive?"

"Yes."

I sighed, relieved, and then paused. The sound of its speech vibrating against my skin. This was its true voice. I could not only hear at its frequency, but I saw its tentacles quiver as it spoke. And I could understand it. Before, it had just looked like their tentacles were quivering for no reason.

"Was it the sting?" I asked.

"No," it said. "That is something else. You understand, because you truly are what you say you are—a harmonizer."

I didn't care to understand. Not at the moment.

"Your tentacle," I said. "Your *okuoko*." It hung straight, still pink but now translucent like the others.

"The rest was used to help several of our sick," it said. "Your people will be remembered by my people."

The more it spoke, the less monstrous its voice sounded. I took another step.

"Are you ready?" Okwu asked.

I was. I left the *edan* behind with my other things.

~

I was still weak from the landing, but this had to happen fast. I don't know how they broke the news of their presence to Oomza Uni authorities, but they must have. Otherwise, how would we be able to leave the ship during the brightest part of the day?

I understood the plan as soon as Okwu and the chief came to my room. I followed them down the hallway. We did not pass through the dining room where so many had been brutally killed, and I was glad. But as we passed the entrance, I saw all the Meduse in there. The bodies were all gone. The chairs and tables were all stacked on one side of the large room as if a windstorm had swept through it. Between the transparent folds and tentacles, I thought I glimpsed someone in the red flowing uniform of the pilot, but I wasn't sure.

"You know what you will say," the chief said. Not a question, but a statement. And within the statement, a threat.

I wore my best red shirt and wrapper, made from the threads of well-fed silkworms. I'd bought it for my first day of class at Oomza Uni, but this was a more important occasion. And I'd used fresh *otjize* on my skin and to thicken my plaited hair even more. As I'd palm rolled my plaits smooth like the bodies of snakes, I noticed that my hair had grown about an inch since I'd left home. This was odd. I looked at the thick wiry new growth, admiring its dark brown color before pressing the *otjize* onto it, making it red. There was a tingling sensation on my scalp as I worked the *otjize* in and my head ached. I was exhausted. I held my *otjize*-covered hands to my nose and inhaled the scent of home.

Years ago, I had snuck out to the lake one night with some other girls and we'd all washed and scrubbed off all our *otjize* using the lake's salty water. It took us half the night. Then we'd stared at each other horrified by what we'd done. If any man saw us, we'd be ruined for life. If our parents saw us, we'd all be beaten and that would only be a fraction of the punishment. Our families and people we knew would think us mentally unstable when they heard, and that too would ruin our chances of marriage.

But above all this, outside of the horror of what we'd done, we all felt an awesome glorious . . . shock. Our hair hung in thick clumps, black in the moonlight. Our skin glistened, dark brown. *Glistened*. And there had been a breeze that night and it felt amazing on our exposed skin. I thought of this as I applied the *otjize* to my new growth, covering up the dark brown color of my hair. What if I washed it all off now? I was the first of my people to come to Oomza Uni, would the people here even know the difference? But Okwu and the chief came minutes later and there was no time. Plus, really, this was Oomza Uni, someone would have researched and known of my people. And that person would know I was naked if I washed all my *otjize* off . . . and crazy.

I didn't want to do it anyway, I thought as I walked behind Okwu and the chief. There were soldiers waiting at the doorway; both were human and I wondered what point they were trying to make by doing that. Just like the photos in the books I read, they wore all-blue kaftans and no shoes.

"You first," the chief growled, moving behind me. I

felt one of its tentacles, heavy and smooth, shove me softly in the back right where I'd been stung. The soreness there caused me to stand up taller. And then more softly in a voice that only tickled my ear with its strange vibration. "Look strong, girl."

Following the soldiers and followed by two Meduse, I stepped onto the surface of another planet for the first time in my life. My scalp was still tingling, and this added to the magical sensation of being so far from home. The first thing I noticed was the smell and weight of the air when I walked off the ship. It smelled jungly, green, heavy with leaves. The air was full of *water*. It was just like the air in the ship's plant-filled breathing chambers!

I parted my lips and inhaled it as I followed the soldiers down the open black walkway. Behind me, I heard the Meduse, pluming out and sucking in gas. Softly, though, unlike on the ship. We were walking toward a great building, the ship port.

"We will take you to the Oomza Uni Presidential Building," one of the soldiers said in to me in perfect Khoush. He looked up at the Meduse and I saw a crease of worry wrinkle his brow. "I don't know . . . their language. Can you . . ."

I nodded.

He looked about twenty-five and was dark brown skinned like me, but unlike the men of my people, his skin was naked, his hair shaven low, and he was quite short, standing a head shorter than me. "Do you mind swift transport?"

I turned and translated for Okwu and the chief.

"These people are primitive," the chief responded. But it and Okwu agreed to board the shuttle.

~

The room's wall and floor were a light blue, the large open windows letting in sunshine and a warm breeze. There were ten professors, one from each of the ten university departments. They sat, stood, hovered, and crouched behind a long table of glass. Against every wall were soldiers wearing blue uniforms of cloth, color, and light. There were so many different types of people in the room that I found it hard to concentrate. But I had to or there would be more death.

The one who spoke for all the professors looked like one of the sand people's gods and I almost laughed. It was like a spider made of wind, gray and undulating, here and not quite there. When it spoke, it was in a whisper that I could clearly hear despite the fact that I was several feet away. And it spoke in the language of the Meduse.

It introduced itself as something that sounded like "Haras" and said, "Tell me what you need to tell me."

And then all attention was suddenly on me.

~

"None of you have ever seen anyone like me," I said. "I come from a people who live near a small salty lake on the edge of a desert. On my people's land, fresh water, water humans can drink, is so little that we do not use it to bathe as so many others do. We wash with *otjize*, a mix of red clay from our land and oils from our local flowers."

Several of the human professors looked at each other and chuckled. One of the large insectile people clicked its mandibles. I frowned, flaring my nostrils. It was the first time I'd received treatment similar to the way my people were treated on Earth by the Khoush. In a way, this set me at ease. People were people, everywhere. These professors were just like anyone else.

"This was my first time leaving the home of my parents. I had never even left my own city, let alone my planet Earth. Days later, in the blackness of space, everyone on my ship but the pilot was killed, many right before my eyes, by a people at war with those who view my own people as near slaves." I waited for this to sink in, then continued. "You've never seen the Meduse, either. Only studied them . . . from afar. I know. I have read about them too." I stepped forward. "Or maybe some of you or your students have studied the stinger you have in the weapons museum up close."

I saw several of them look at each other. Some murmured to one another. Others, I did not know well enough to tell what they were doing. As I spoke, I fell into a rhythm, a meditative state very much like my math-induced ones. Except I was fully present, and before long tears were falling from my eyes. I told them in detail about watching Heru's chest burst open, desperately grabbing food, staying in that room waiting to die, the *edan* saving me and not knowing how or why or what.

I spoke of Okwu and how my *otjize* had really been what saved me. I spoke of the Meduse's cold exactness, focus, violence, sense of honor, and willingness to listen. I said things that I didn't know I'd thought about or comprehended. I found words I didn't even know I knew. And eventually, I told them how they could satisfy the Meduse and prevent a bloodbath in which everyone would lose.

I was sure they would agree. These professors were educated beyond anything I could imagine. Thoughtful. Insightful. United. Individual. The Meduse chief came forward and spoke its piece, as well. It was angry, but thorough, eloquent with a sterile logic. "If you do not give it to us willingly, we have the right to take back what was brutally stolen from us without provocation," the chief said.

After the chief spoke, the professors discussed among themselves for over an hour. They did not retreat to a separate room to do this. They did it right before the chief, Okwu, and me. They moved from the glass table and stood in a group.

Okwu, the chief, and I just stood there. Back in my home, the elders were always stoic and quiet and they always discussed everything in private. It must have been the same for the Meduse, because Okwu's tentacles shuddered and it said, "What kind of people are these?"

"Let them do the right thing," the chief said.

Feet away from us, beyond the glass table, these professors were shouting with anger, sometimes guffawing with glee, flicking antennae in each other's faces, making ear-popping clicks to get the attention of colleagues. One professor, about the size of my head, flew from one part of the group to the other, producing webs of gray light that slowly descended on the group. This chaotic method of madness would decide whether I would live or die.

I caught bits and pieces of the discussion about Meduse history and methods, the mechanics of the Third Fish, the scholars who'd brought the stinger. Okwu and the chief didn't seem to mind hovering there waiting. However, my legs soon grew tired and I sat down right there on the blue floor.

~

Finally, the professors quieted and took their places at the glass table again. I stood up, my heart seeming to pound in my mouth, my palms sweaty. I glanced at the chief and felt even more nervous; its *okuoko* were vibrating and its blue color was deeper, almost glowing. When I looked at Okwu, where its *okuoko* hung, I caught a glimpse of the white of its stinger, ready to strike.

The spiderlike Haras raised two front legs and spoke in the language of the Meduse and said, "On behalf of all the people of Oomza Uni and on behalf of Oomza University, I apologize for the actions of a group of our own in taking the stinger from you, Chief Meduse. The scholars who did this will be found, expelled, and exiled. Museum specimen of such prestige are highly prized at our university, however such things must only be acquired with permission from the people to whom they belong. Oomza protocol is based on honor, respect, wisdom, and knowledge. We will return it to you immediately."

My legs grew weak and before I knew it, I was sitting back on the floor. My head felt heavy and tingly, my thoughts scattered. "I'm sorry," I said, in the language I'd spoken all my life. I felt something press my back, steadying me. Okwu.

"I am all right," I said, pushing my hands to the floor and standing back up. But Okwu kept a tentacle to my back.

The one named Haras continued. "Binti, you have made your people proud and I'd personally like to welcome you to Oomza Uni." It motioned one of its limbs toward the human woman beside it. She looked Khoush and wore tight-fitting green garments that clasped every part of her body, from neck to toe. "This is Okpala. She is in our mathematics department. When you are settled, aside from taking classes with her, you will study your *edan* with her. According to Okpala, what you did is impossible."

I opened my mouth to speak, but Okpala put up a hand and I shut my mouth.

"We have one request," Haras said. "We of Oomza Uni wish Okwu to stay behind as the first Meduse student to attend the university and as a showing of allegiance between Oomza Uni governments and the Meduse and a renewal of the pact between human and Meduse."

I heard Okwu rumble behind me, then the chief was speaking up. "For the first time in my own lifetime, I am learning something completely outside of core beliefs," the chief said. "Who'd have thought that a place harboring human beings could carry such honor and foresight." It paused and then said, "I will confer with my advisors before I make my decision."

The chief was pleased. I could hear it in its voice. I looked around me. No one from my tribe. At once, I felt both part of something historic and very alone. Would my family even comprehend it all when I explained it to them? Or would they just fixate on the fact that I'd almost died, was now too far to return home and had left them in order to make the "biggest mistake of my life"?

I swayed on my feet, a smile on my face.

"Binti," the one named Okpala said. "What will you do now?"

"What do you mean?" I asked. "I want to study mathematics and currents. Maybe create a new type of astrolabe. The *edan*, I want to study that and . . ."

"Yes," she said. "That is true, but what about your home? Will you ever return?"

"Of course," I said. "Eventually, I will visit and . . ."

"I have studied your people," she said. "They don't like outsiders."

"I'm not an outsider," I said, with a twinge of irritation. "I am . . ." And that's when it caught my eye. My hair was rested against my back, weighed down by the *otjize*, but as I'd gotten up, one lock had come to rest on my shoulder. I felt it rub against the front of my shoulder and I *saw* it now.

I frowned, not wanting to move. Before the realization hit me, I knew to drop into meditation, treeing out of desperation. I held myself in there for a moment, equations flying through my mind, like wind and sand. Around me, I heard movement and, still treeing, I saw that the soldiers were leaving the room. The professors were getting up, talking among themselves in their various ways. All except Okpala. She was looking right at me.

I slowly lifted up one of my locks and brought it forward I rubbed off the *ojtize*. It glowed a strong deep blue like the sky back on earth on a clear day, like Okwu and so many of the other Meduse, like the uniforms of the Oomza Uni soldiers. And it was translucent. Soft, but tough. I touched the top of my head and pressed. They felt the same and . . . I felt my hand touching them. The tingling sensation was gone. My hair was no longer hair. There was a ringing in my ear as I began to breathe heavily, still in meditation. I wanted to tear off my clothes and inspect every part of my body. To see what else that sting had changed. It had not been a sting. A sting would have torn out my insides, as it did for Heru.

"Only those," Okwu said. "Nothing else."

"This is why I understand you?" I flatly asked. Talking while in meditation was like softly whispering from a hole deep in the ground. I was looking up from a cool dark place.

"Yes."

"Why?"

"Because you had to understand us and it was the only way," Okwu said.

"And you needed to prove to them that you were truly our ambassador, not prisoner," the chief said. It paused. "I will return to the ship; we will make our decision about Okwu." It turned to leave and then turned back. "Binti, you will forever hold the highest honor among the Meduse. My destiny is stronger for leading me to you." Then it left.

I stood there, in my strange body. If I hadn't been deep in meditation I would have screamed and screamed. I was so far from home.

~

I'm told that news of what had happened spread across all Oomza Uni within minutes. It was said that a human tribal female from a distant blue planet saved the university from Meduse terrorists by sacrificing her blood and using her unique gift of mathematical harmony and ancestral magic. "Tribal": that's what they called humans from ethnic groups too remote and "uncivilized" to regularly send students to attend Oomza Uni.

Over the next two days, I learned that people viewed my reddened dark skin and strange hair with wonder.

And when they saw me with Okwu, they grew tense and quiet, moving away. Where they saw me as a fascinating exotic human, they saw Okwu as a dangerous threat. Okwu was of a warlike people who, up until now, had only been viewed with fear among people from all over. Okwu enjoyed its infamy, whereas I just wanted to find a quiet desert to walk into so I could study in peace.

"All people fear decisive, proud honor," Okwu proclaimed.

We were in one of the Weapons City libraries, staring at the empty chamber where the chief's stinger had been kept. A three-hour transport from Math City, Weapons City was packed with activity on every street and crowded with sprawling flat gray buildings made of stone. Beneath each of these structures were inverted buildings that extended at least a half-mile underground where only those students, researchers, and professors involved knew what was being invented, tested, or destroyed. After the meeting, this was where they'd taken me, the chief, and Okwu for the retrieval of the stinger.

We'd been escorted by a person who looked like a small green child with roots for a head, who I later learned was the head professor of Weapons City. He was the one who went into the five-by-five-foot case made of thick clear crystal and opened it. The stinger was placed atop a slab of crystal and looked like a sharp tusk of ice.

The chief slowly approached the case, extended an *okuoko*, and then let out a large bluish plume of gas the moment its *okuoko* touched the stinger. I'll never forget the way the chief's body went from blue to clear the moment the stinger became a part of it again. Only a blue line remained at the point of demarcation where it had reattached—a scar that would always remind it of what human beings of Oomza Uni had done to it for the sake of research and academics.

Afterward, just before the chief and the others boarded the Third Fish that would take them back to their own ship just outside the atmosphere, upon Okwu's request, I knelt before the chief and placed its stinger on my lap. It was heavy and it felt like a slab of solid water and the edge at its tip looked like it could slice into another universe. I smeared a dollop of my *otjize* on the blue scar where it had reattached. After a minute, I wiped some of it away. The blue scar was gone. Their chief was returned to its full royal translucence, they had the half jar of *otjize* Okwu had taken from me, which healed their flesh like magic, and they were leaving one of their own as the first Meduse to study at the great Oomza University. The Meduse left Oomza Uni happier and better off than when they'd arrived.

~

My *otjize*. Yes, there is a story there. Weeks later, after I'd started classes and people had finally started to leave me be, opting to simply stare and gossip in silence instead, I ran out of *otjize*. For days, I'd known it would happen. I'd found a sweet-smelling oil of the same chemical makeup in the market. A black flower that grew in a series of nearby caverns produced the oil. But a similar clay was much harder to find. There was a forest not far from my dorm, across the busy streets, just beyond one of the classroom buildings. I'd never seen anyone go into it, but there was a path opening.

That evening, before dark, I walked in there. I walked fast, ignoring all the stares and grateful when the presence of people tapered off the closer I got to the path entrance. I carried my satchel with my astrolabe, a bag of nuts, my *edan* in my hands, cool and small. I squeezed my *edan* as I left the road and stepped onto the path. The forest seemed to swallow me within a few steps and I could no longer see the purpling sky. My skin felt near naked, the layer of *otjize* I wore was so thin.

I frowned, hesitating for a moment. We didn't have such places where I came from and the denseness of the trees, all the leaves, the small buzzing creatures, made me feel like the forest was choking me. But then I looked at the ground. I looked right there, at my sandaled feet and found precisely what I needed.

I made the *otjize* that night. I mixed it and then let it sit in the strong sunshine for the next day. I didn't go to class, nor did I eat that day. In the evening, I went to the dorm and showered and did that which my people rarely do: I washed with water. As I let the water run through my hair and down my face, I wept. This was all I had left of my homeland and it was being washed into the runnels that would feed the trees outside my dorm.

When I finished, I stood there, away from the running stream of water that flowed from the ceiling. Slowly, I reached up. I touched my "hair." The *okuoko* were soft but firm and slippery with wetness. They touched my back, soft and slick. I shook them, feeling them *otjize*-free for the first time.

I shut my eyes and prayed to the Seven; I hadn't done this since arriving on the planet. I prayed to my living parents and ancestors. I opened my eyes. It was time to call home. Soon.

I peeked out of the washing space. I shared the space with five other human students. One of them just happened to be leaving as I peeked out. As soon as he was gone, I grabbed my wrapper and came out. I wrapped it around my waist and I looked at myself in the large mirror. I looked for a very very long time. Not at my dark brown skin, but where my hair had been. The *okuoko* were a soft transparent blue with darker blue dots at their tips. They grew out of my head as if they'd been doing that all my life, so natural looking that I couldn't say they were ugly. They were just a little longer than my hair had been, hanging just past my backside, and they were thick as sizable snakes.

There were ten of them and I could no longer braid them into my family's code pattern as I had done with my own hair. I pinched one and felt the pressure. Would they grow like hair? *Were* they hair? I could ask Okwu, but I wasn't ready to ask it anything. Not yet. I quickly ran to my room and sat in the sun and let them dry.

Ten hours later, when dark finally fell, it was time. I'd bought the container at the market; it was made from the shed exoskeleton of students who sold them for spending money. It was clear like one of Okwu's tentacles and dyed red. I'd packed it with the fresh *otjize*, which now looked thick and ready.

I pressed my right index and middle finger together and was about to dig out the first dollop when I hesitated, suddenly incredibly unsure. What if my fingers passed right through it like liquid soap? What if what I'd harvested from the forest wasn't clay at all? What if it was hard like stone?

I pulled my hand away and took a deep breath. If I couldn't make *otjize* here, then I'd have to . . . change. I touched one of my tentacle-like locks and felt a painful pressure in my chest as my mind tried to take me to a place I wasn't ready to go to. I plunged my two fingers into my new concoction . . . and scooped it up. I spread it on my flesh. Then I wept.

I went to see Okwu in its dorm. I was still unsure what to call those who lived in this large gas-filled spherical complex. When you entered, it was just one great space where plants grew on the walls and hung from the ceiling. There were no individual rooms, and people who looked like Okwu in some ways but different in others walked across the expansive floor, up the walls, on the ceiling. Somehow, when I came to the front entrance, Okwu would always come within the next few minutes. It would always emit a large plume of gas as it readjusted to the air outside.

"You look well," it said, as we walked down the walkway. We both loved the walkway because of the winds the warm clear seawater created as it rushed by below.

I smiled. "I *feel* well."

"When did you make it?"

"Over the last two suns," I said.

"I'm glad," it said. "You were beginning to fade."

It held up an *okuoko*. "I was working with a yellow

current to use in one of my classmate's body tech," it said.

"Oh," I said, looking at its burned flesh.

We paused, looking down at the rushing waters. The relief I'd felt at the naturalness, the trueness of the *otjize* immediately started waning. *This* was the real test. I rubbed some *otjize* from my arm and them took Okwu's *okuoko* in my hand. I applied the *otjize* and then let the *okuoko* drop as I held my breath. We walked back to my dorm. My *otjize* from Earth had healed Okwu and then the chief. It would heal many others. The *otjize* created by my people, mixed with my homeland. This was the foundation of the Meduse's respect for me. Now all of it was gone. I was someone else. Not even fully Himba anymore. What would Okwu think of me now?

When we got to my dorm, we stopped.

"I know what you are thinking," Okwu said.

"I know you Meduse," I said. "You're people of honor, but you're firm and rigid. And traditional." I felt sorrow wash over and I sobbed, covering my face with my hand. Feeling my *otjize* smear beneath it. "But you've become my friend," I said. When I brought my hand away, my palm was red with *otjize*. "You are all I have here. I don't know how it happened, but you are . . ."

"You will call your family and have them," Okwu said.

I frowned and stepped away from Okwu. "So callous," I whispered.

"Binti," Okwu said. It plumed out gas, in what I knew was a laugh. "Whether you carry the substance that can heal and bring life back to my people or not, I am your friend. I am honored to know you." It shook its *okuoko*, making one of them vibrate. I yelped when I felt the vibration in one of mine.

"What is that?" I shouted, holding up my hands.

"It means we are family through battle," it said. "You are the first to join our family in this way in a long time. We do not like humans."

I smiled.

He held up an *okuoko*. "Show it to me tomorrow," I said, doubtfully.

"Tomorrow will be the same," it said.

When I rubbed off the *otjize* the burn was gone.

~

I sat in the silence of my room looking at my *edan* as I sent out a signal to my family with my astrolabe. Outside was dark and I looked into the sky, at the stars, knowing the pink one was home. The first to answer was my mother.

Acknowledgments

I'd like to thank my daughter, Anyaugo, for essentially coming up with the plot of this novella. When you get stuck, ask a plucky imaginative eleven-year-old what happens next in the story; you'll be unstuck in no time. Many thanks to my Tor.com editor, Lee Harris (one of the prime visionaries of Tor.com's novella program), and my agent, Don Maass (for knowing precisely the right place for this story). Thanks to my beta reader, Angel Maynard, for all her encouragement. Lastly, I'd like to thank a jellyfish, someone close to me with deep traditional and tribal beliefs, the lovely Himba people of Namibia, and the futuristic ancient lands of the United Arab Emirates for inspiring me to explore outer space.

About the Author

Photograph by Anyaugo Okorafor-Mbachu

Nnedi Okorafor was born in the United States to two Igbo (Nigerian) immigrant parents. She holds a Ph.D. in English and is an associate professor of creative writing, currently teaching at the University at Buffalo. She has been the winner of many awards for her short stories and young adult books, including the Wole Soyinka Africa Prize for Literature, the Macmillan Writer's Prize for Africa, Le Prix Imaginales (Best Translated Novel), the Carl Brandon Parallax Award, the Black Excellence Award for Outstanding Achievement in Literature, and the Strange Horizons Readers Choice Award for Nonfiction. She has also been a finalist for the *Essence* Magazine Literary Award, Tiptree Award, a British Science Fiction

Association Award (Best Novel), and the Theodore Sturgeon Award. She was also a nominee for the NAACP Imagine Award, among others. Nnedi's stories are inspired by her Nigerian heritage, her many trips there and her travels around the world. Her first published adult novel, *Who Fears Death*, won the World Fantasy Award for Best Novel. Nnedi lives in Illinois with her daughter, Anyaugo, and family.

TOR·COM

Science fiction. Fantasy.
The universe.
And related subjects.

★

More than just a publisher's website, Tor.com
is a venue for **original fiction, comics,** and
discussion of the entire field of SF and fantasy,
in all media and from all sources. Visit our site
today — and join the conversation yourself.